Presented to

_____

By

_____

On the Occasion of

_____

THE BLACK & WHITE
Rainbow

WRITTEN BY

JOHN TRENT ◆ JUDY LOVE

ILLUSTRATED BY

WATERBROOK
PRESS

THE BLACK AND WHITE RAINBOW
PUBLISHED BY WATERBROOK PRESS
5446 North Academy Boulevard, Suite 200
Colorado Springs, Colorado 80918
A division of Random House, Inc.

ISBN 1-57856-036-5

Published in association with the literary agency of
Alive Communications, Inc.,
1465 Kelly Johnson Blvd., Suite 320,
Colorado Springs, Colorado 80920

Printed in the United States of America
1999—First Edition

10 9 8 7 6 5 4 3 2 1

Dedication

❖

This book is dedicated to Amber, Wade, and April McCombs

(and, of course, their dad and mom, Todd and Denise).

Thank you for shining God's love and light on the Trent Family.

We love you!

Chapter One:
HOW IT HAPPENED

Mooseberry thought it was just about the most perfect summer's day he had ever seen — the kind of day picnics were made for, and kites and kids long for. Warm, yellow sunlight filled the Forest, showering sparkles on the leaves of the trees. Flowers were bursting with reds and yellows and splashes of blue. The grass seemed like an ocean of green waves tossing in the warm breeze.

Yet even on such a delightful day, not everything was perfect in the Forest. In fact...

…in the last month, six of Mooseberry's friends had disappeared! Twelve sock-footed Ferrets had been seen sneaking around the Forest, and they were suspected of having captured the Mice. There were rumors that the cute but misguided Ferrets had carried the captured Mice away to the forest hideout of an unusually large and unpleasant Mole named Monty.

So now Mooseberry had started roaming the Forest to protect his fellow Mice. Although he was small, without a doubt Mooseberry was one of the bravest Mice in the Forest. His nose and ears were always on alert, and every time he spotted a hiding Ferret, Mooseberry warned the other Mice by blowing a large, shiny whistle. The shrill, ear-splitting sound made the Ferrets cover their little ears and run away.

As that beautiful summer's day
came to an end, Mooseberry continued his Forest patrol under a golden
sunset sky, making sure all the Mice
were safe and snug in their homes. Yet
even that brave Mouse and his whistle
couldn't chase away the darkness that was
coming.

For that very night — sometime between
"lay me down" prayers and first morning light
— something terrible happened.

The next morning, every Mouse in every Mouse house or Mouse apartment awoke to a world *without a single bit of color!*

Just imagine a world where every teddy bear's fur is black or white or gray—but never brown. Where every doll wears a gown as pale as ash or as dark as midnight—but never blue or yellow or pink. Where a favorite bicycle that was once shiny green is now a dreary gray. And where the red-checked tablecloth in the kitchen looks like a black and white checkerboard.

If it had been Christmas (which, thankfully, it wasn't), all the lights on all the Christmas trees would have twinkled black and white!

The whole world had lost its color. Even —terror of terrors—Saturday morning cartoons were in black and white! Who could imagine something so terrible?

The Animals' Forest world stayed salt-and-pepper colored, day after day. With sad eyes and sinking spirits, all the Mice missed the blue waters of their river, the orange sunrises and pink sunsets, and the songs of their good friends the Red-Breasted Robins, who were now too sad to sing because they had become *Black-Breasted Robins* instead.

Everyone quickly grew tired of gooey gray peanut butter, strawberry jam that looked like sticky tar, white lemonade, and popsicles that looked the same no matter what flavor.

But the day it rained, the Forest Animals discovered something much, much worse. After large gray raindrops fell all morning, the dark clouds finally pulled back in the late afternoon. Just like always, a huge rainbow appeared — almost close enough to touch. Only this wasn't a beautiful rainbow like the last one you've seen…

This was a black and white rainbow!

At this tragic sight, the Mice stood below
the rainbow and wept. "Who took away all our
colors?" they cried. "We want the old rainbow!
We want back our beautiful world!"

With his sensitive heart, Mooseberry missed
the rainbow's beautiful colors even more than everyone else.

Perhaps that's why, as he walked home that afternoon with his head hanging low, he wasn't thinking of
whistles or Ferrets…until it was too late!

From behind the trees near Mooseberry's house, twelve Ferrets fell upon him. Although he bravely resisted, both Mooseberry and his whistle were soon tied up and carried off…just like his friends before him.

The Ferrets carried him through the Forest to the Mole's backwoods hideout.

Nearby stood something that caused Mooseberry's heart to skip a beat and made his fur stand on end. It was a giant slingshot, as big as a house!

"Well," said Monty, who was calmly eating his lunch, "if it isn't Mouse Missile Number Seven!"

"What do you mean?" asked Mooseberry, as the Ferrets strapped him into the stretchy part of the giant slingshot.

"Where do you think your six friends went?" chuckled the Mole, who was talking with his mouth full of food. "You and your whistle have caused me enough trouble. You're about to take a trip so fast and so far that you'll never find your way back to this Forest."

"Wait!" cried Mooseberry as the Ferrets began pulling back on the slingshot. "Tell me first: Was it *you?* Are *you* the one who stole the color from our world?"

Wiping his mouth with a huge napkin, the Mole smiled his smirkiest smile. "I see you're not only a brave mouse but a smart one as well. Yes, I stole it all! I absolutely *hate* light and bright colors. They hurt my eyes. I'm tired of staying inside that dark and damp hole all the time. Now I can come out all day long whenever I want. And I can be King of the Forest, just as I always wanted!"

He snarled at Mooseberry. "And that's why I need *you* out of the way, just as I got rid of your friends!"

Monty quickly commanded the Ferrets:

"READY!…"

"Wait!" shouted Mooseberry.

"AIM!…"

"No!" Mooseberry cried. *"Please don't!"*

"FIRE!"
With a snap and a zing, Mooseberry was hurled high
into the sky!

As he flew over the black and white rainbow, he saw the Mice down below, still weeping together.

Quickly he called out, "It was Monty the Mole! MONTY STOLE ALL THE COLOR-R-R-R-R-R-S!"

But that's all he could say. In the time it takes you to blink your eyes (you might try a blink right now just to see how fast that is!), Mooseberry's friends and all the Forest disappeared from his sight.

Farther and farther he soared until he was out over the open sea. Mooseberry wanted to stay brave, but he shut his eyes tight as he fell toward the cold, gray waters.

Suddenly, instead of landing with a cold splash, Mooseberry thudded into something softer than your pillow!

He had flown right into the sail of a mighty ship, and now he was sliding safely down until he dropped gently onto the deck.

Filled with joy at this surprise rescue, Mooseberry gave a loud cheer — a cheer that ended almost as soon as it started.

Someone — or *something* — was standing over him with a sword! It was a tall, proud creature — and as full of color as a rainbow.

Color!

Mooseberry was seeing so much color, it nearly blinded him.

He squinted his eyes and watched in amazement as the tall creature touched his sword to his cap and said, "I am Captain Chameleon, and I'm glad you're finally here!"

"AND SO ARE WE!" Mooseberry heard several voices say.

Rushing across the deck to greet him were his friends — the six Mouse Missiles that had been launched before him.

There were hugs and handshakes all around, but Mooseberry stood in a daze, too astounded to talk. He turned to Captain Chameleon with eyes that begged for an explanation.

With a smile the Captain grabbed Mooseberry's shoulders and said, "The Ruler of All, the Great King Across the Sea, has sent me to rescue you and your friends from drowning."

Then he lowered his voice to a whisper: "And now we've no time to lose. We're sailing back to where you Mouse Missiles came from. And *you*, Mooseberry, will lead your friends in bringing back the color to your world."

"*Me?*" Mooseberry asked. "But how?"

Chapter Two:

By the time the ship had crossed the sea and was sailing up the river to the Forest, Captain Chameleon had explained the plan.

"There is a way to win back all the color," he told the seven Mice. "You'll need *four* secret weapons. I'll give you these weapons *after* you've gathered all your families and Forest friends together for a Great Council at the Meadow."

When they reached the Forest, the seven rescued Mice ran in every direction to tell all their friends and families.

Fortunately, Monty the Mole had given the Ferrets the day off, so they did not see everyone sneaking toward the Meadow.

Soon the Great Council was gathered. A hush swept over the Meadow as Captain Chameleon stood up in the center of the crowd. "Dear Friends," he called out, "listen carefully to this…

"Long, long ago, in a time before the very first rainbow, many men and beasts in this world chose darkness over light. Wrong instead of right. Curses instead of blessing.

"'Those days of darkness were cut short by a Great Flood. But the Ruler of All provided a great ship, called an Ark, as a way of escape for those who loved Him....

"He also gave them His rainbow full of color and light, and He promised that no flood would ever again sweep over all the earth....

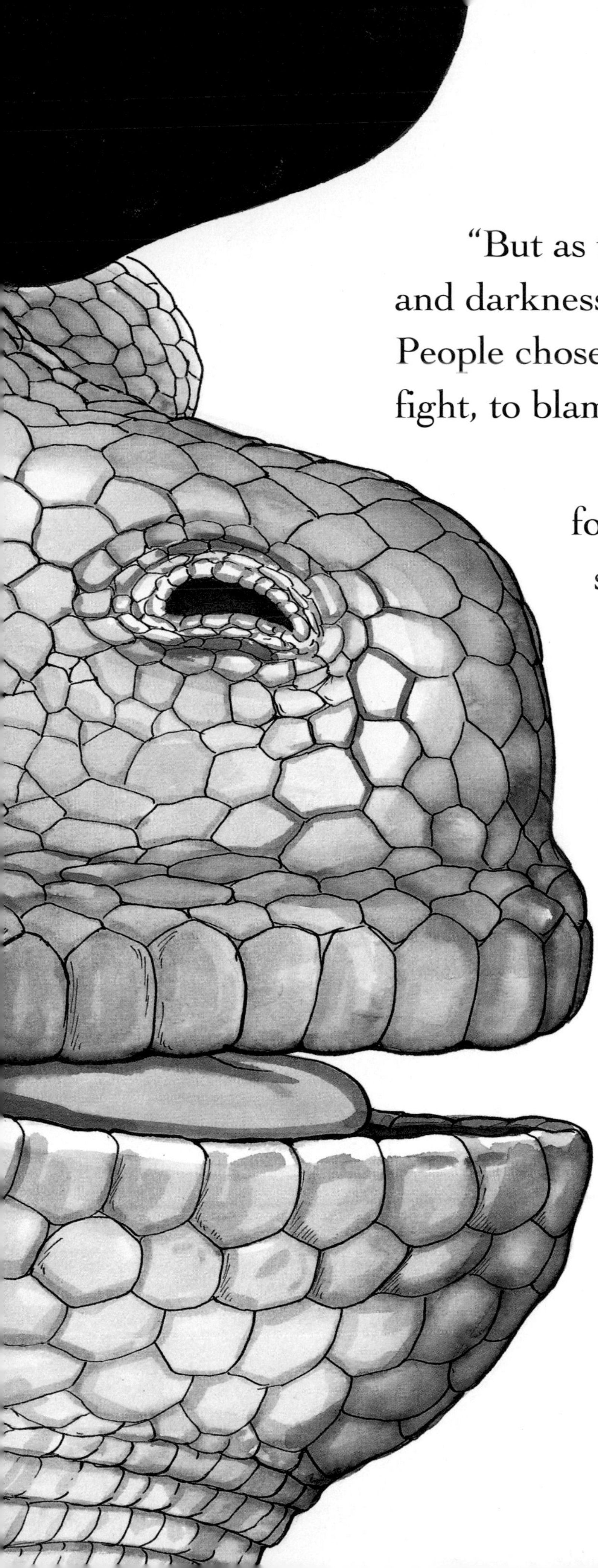

"But as the years passed, shadows
and darkness again crept over the world.
People chose once more to hate and to
fight, to blame and to hide.

"So, to break the darkness
forever, the Ruler of All did
something even better
than before....

"One winter's night, a bright light shown down from heaven into a stable where a tiny, newborn baby was lying. This baby was the precious Son of the Ruler of All. He Himself was the very Light of the World, so bright and full of color that His love could push aside any shadow and break any curse.

"Today, my Forest Friends, I bring you His weapons. When you use these weapons with the King's love, they can bring color and light back to your world.

"Four of the King's weapons I'll give you today.
Each one can help drive the darkness away!"

Then the Captain called Mooseberry's best friend, Elkenberry, to the front of the crowd.

And he said to her, "The first weapon is something that you, Elkenberry, already use with great skill.

"Everyone knows how beautiful you are. You're a Mouse of kindness and beauty. And what makes you beautiful is how helpful and cheerful you are to everyone in the Forest. Not long ago you visited a sick Rabbit and made him laugh. One day you prayed for a Turtle with a twisted neck, and that helped him so much. And your happy songs have cheered up even the saddest of the Robins."

And as the Chameleon continued to praise the small Mouse, something miraculous happened....

Elkenberry's cheeks began glowing bright red (she was embarrassed to be singled out for such praise). Then, as everyone gasped, her shawl turned pink and her ballet slippers (which were her quietest shoes for sneaking past Ferrets) turned brilliant red.

Now everyone realized that the first weapon was not a sword or a slingshot, but simply *speaking words of blessing*. By saying words full of love and encouragement, the Animals could bring back the red into their world!

At once, each Forest Animal turned to his friends (or even to strangers) and began telling them how nice they looked, or how kind they had been, or what a good cook or fine student or loyal friend they were. Mooseberry and his six Mouse Missile friends were talking the most, showing everyone how to use this new weapon.

All over the Meadow, words of blessing were being spoken, and shirts and sweaters and belts and bonnets and even eyeglass frames were turning brilliant shades of red.

"Quiet now!" called Captain Chameleon, after lots of blessing words had been spoken. Then he called for Mr. Moose to come forward as he shared a second rhyme:

A second weapon have I brought—
One you must treasure and use a lot.

"A second way to bring color back to your world is by doing something the King's Son did every day with those He loved. And it's something *you*, Mr. Moose, can teach us much about."

"*I can?*" said the Moose.

"Of course," replied the Captain. "The King's Own Son *served* others, just as you serve others and bring light to their lives. One look at your antlers shows everybody that!"

It was true. Moose's antlers were covered with Birds, because Moose offered his head as a rest stop and hotel to every tired Bird in the Forest.

And now as Captain Chameleon spoke, those dozens of gray birds perched in Moose's antlers watched their feathers turn a beautiful shade of yellow!

Quickly, Mooseberry and the other Mouse Missiles began helping everyone in the Meadow find a way to serve one another. They fetched a chair for Grandmother Mouse, who was tired of standing. They handed handkerchiefs to a family of Squirrels with the sneezes. And they helped a Centipede tie his shoe and his shoe and his shoe and his shoe and...

Finally, Captain Chameleon spoke again:

"Saying and serving are two ways to bless;
There's also another that brings out God's best."

In a flash, Captain Chameleon reached into his cape. With one hand he pulled out a serving of scrumptious three-layer chocolate fudge cake. With the other hand he pulled out a plate of melt-in-your-mouth strawberry cake with thick, creamy icing.

He handed Mooseberry the two plates and asked him NOT to take a bite. Instead, Mooseberry was to pass one piece of cake to each of the twin Raccoons standing on either side of him. They, in turn, were to pass the cakes on to the next person.

Now, if you'd just eaten three helpings of your favorite dinner, passing scrumptious cake on to someone else might not be difficult. But Mooseberry had not eaten a bite all day long. His ears heard the words "Pass on the cake." But his eyes and his mouth and his tummy said, "Just a bit of icing…or one little bite…or two…or maybe two pieces…"

Mooseberry finally gathered all his strength and did as he was asked. He passed the cake to the Raccoons. But instead of going hungry…

…suddenly, into his hands popped two more plates with two pieces of cake: one a deep, dark brown chocolate and the other with beautiful strawberry pink icing!

The same thing happened when the Raccoons passed their cake on; the more they shared, the more they were served themselves.

Suddenly, the Meadow turned into a sharing place —and a more colorful place as well! For with every act of sharing, pinks and greens and blues and browns appeared!

With all the Forest Animals' *saying* and *serving* and *sharing,* all the colors of the Meadow had come back!

Or at least that's what everyone *thought.*

Chapter Three:
THE KING'S COLOR

All the Forest Animals would have been more than happy to stay in the Great Meadow and receive more hugs and helps and pieces of cake — but the shriek of a whistle stopped all the blessings.

Captain Chameleon had blown Mooseberry's whistle, and now he said to them, "Whether small or tall, you can all *say* and *serve* and *share*. These are the three weapons you've used to change this Meadow. But now you've got a Forest to fill up with love and light and color!"

With a shout and a song, Mooseberry and the other Mouse Missiles led the way out of the Meadow and in every direction through the Forest.

When Mooseberry and his friends came across the Ferrets, instead of scolding or chasing them, the Forest Animals *blessed* them.

"Good day!" said Mooseberry to the Ferrets. "Did I ever tell you what shiny coats of fur you have?"

Another Mouse shared a piece of strawberry cake with a Ferret.

And a Rabbit gave a Ferret a warm hug.

With all this blessing, the sky became bluer, the sunshine dazzled with more gold, and the trees all around grew a deeper shade of green.

Soon all of the Ferrets were swamped with Mice *saying, serving,* and *sharing* the same kinds of blessings.

Not far away, a very surprised Mole was squinting his eyes at all this sudden light and brightness. Were those *Mice* he saw running and dancing with the Ferrets, tossing brightly colored Frisbees to one another, painting water-colors together, and playing a game of "I see a color you don't see"?

And could that really be *Mooseberry* in the middle of all this foolishness?

Monty scowled to see the Animals blessing one another with *saying* and *serving* and *sharing*, as they frolicked under a refreshing mist that sprinkled down from cottony clouds far above.

The Mole stormed angrily right into the middle of the celebration. But he wasn't beaten — not by a long shot. He knew something the other Animals didn't.

"You think you've got the best of me!" he shouted in a voice so loud and smug and superior that all the playing and laughing instantly stopped. "But there will always be one color missing from your world. It's right here sewed up tight in my vest pocket. And you will never get it back!

"If you don't believe me, look up at the rainbow. You'll see it's true!"

Sure enough, up in the sky a rainbow had appeared in the mist…with one color missing! In all the joy of seeing so many colors come back, the Animals hadn't noticed that *purple* was nowhere to be found — not in a flower or a sweater or a hat or a pair of shoes. Not even in the rainbow!

Monty raised his voice even louder. "There is nothing you can do to bring purple back. Nothing!"

The Animals hung their heads in sadness. If the Mole had his way, purple would be lost forever.

At that moment Captain Chameleon stepped forward and said, "It's true! Purple is gone. Yet there is a way to get it back, though it won't be easy.

"Remember that I told you there are *four* secret weapons, and so far I have given you only three. There is only one way to bring back the King's color…only one way to once again enjoy the brightness of purple and with it trade light for darkness and blessing for curse."

Captain Chameleon whispered something to Mooseberry and the other Mouse Missiles. Then they whispered it in the ears of the other Forest Animals.

Then the Mole saw something that shocked him.

All the Forest Animals had bowed their heads, and many were on their knees. They were praying!

They were asking the Great King to give them strength to do something *so difficult* that they couldn't do it on their own.

They asked for the King's strength to forgive the one who had hurt them.

And because they asked, the King gave them that power.

Mooseberry and the six Mouse Missiles led the way.
They rushed right up to the Mole and said, "We forgive you,
Monty, for hurting us. And we forgive your Ferrets, too."

Then all the Animals behind them shouted, "We forgive
you, Mole! And we forgive the Ferrets, too!"

Now Elkenberry stepped forward with a gift for Monty.

Still squinting from the bright light, the Mole unwrapped
the paper and opened the box.

It was a huge pair of sunglasses!

After putting them on, he opened his eyes as wide as he could. Now the bright light and colors didn't bother him!

He could never have imagined such a wonderful gift, which came from those who should have been his enemies but who chose instead to love him.

Behind those sunglasses, Monty's eyes filled with tears.

Then, beginning with his big toes and creeping to the top of his Mole head, all of Monty's color came back.

Monty felt his heart growing larger and larger. Suddenly, the color of the King came bursting out of his vest pocket! Purple light shot straight up to the rainbow!

And like a fresh shower in springtime, colors of all kinds rained down on the Forest friends.

It wasn't long before everyone in the Forest said that
Monty the Mole was the kindest, most loving Forest
Animal of all. (For it's true that those who need blessing
the most, often become the best at blessing others.)

And at Christmastime, delivering presents to all the Forest children became a "snap." That's because Mooseberry, Monty, and the Ferrets used the giant slingshot to shower presents everywhere!

A Word to Parents

❧

Whenever I describe *The Black & White Rainbow* to parents, I see their eyes light up. That's because all of us—and, too often, our children—have been hurt by someone, just as Mooseberry and his friends were hurt by Monty the Mole. We've all experienced negative actions or unkind words that drain the color from our world. And many of us have discovered that there's only way to regain that color: forgive the offending person.

For me, this book reflects my relationship with my father. His leaving when I was an infant, and the dark pictures he brought when he came back into my adolescent life, left me feeling cold and dark inside. I carried that darkness for years until I finally met the "Light of the World." In a personal relationship with Jesus, I discovered that those terrible "black and white" pictures from the past didn't have to rob today of its color and light. Life could be as colorful as a rainbow…but not until I forgave my father.

This doesn't mean I excused his actions or ignored the genuine hurt they caused. But I forgave him, just like Jesus had forgiven me. And when I forgave him, I saw him in a different light, just as Mooseberry saw the Mole in a whole new way. A look of compassion, where once there was only hatred. A realization that I had been tied up in knots over hating him. And a glimpse of the wonderful freedom that comes with forgiveness.

For parents who would like to know more about this incredible power to change the negative pictures in your life to positive ones, may I recommend the "grown-up" book on which this storybook is based. It's called *Choosing to Live the Blessing* and is available from WaterBrook Press.

For your children, I pray that this story will provide a "can't miss" look at two things: the amazing power to light up lives by "blessing" others and the incredible importance of forgiving others.

May your life and your child's life be as bright, beautiful, and colorful as God's rainbow!

John Trent, Ph.D.
President, Encouraging Words